Slow Burn In The Wilderness

Renee Hart

Impassioned Romance Books

ISBN-13: 978-1974314867

ISBN-10: 1974314863

Alaska Adventure Romance Books by Renee Hart

A Single Year In The Bush

A Summer Nanny In Fairbanks/
The River Home

Homer: End Of The Road

Together In The Wild

Something Wild in Anchorage/
Touched By The Northern Lights

Yesterday Island

Slow Burn In The Wilderness

Table of Contents

Slow Burn In The Wilderness

An Alaska Adventure Novella

Description

Trevor has come to the Alaskan Bush to fight wildfires.

His job takes him to remote areas for long stretches of time. With no family in his life, Trevor is alone.

When he arrives at the new camp he doesn't know what to make of his new boss, a wisp of a woman with auburn hair. The other crew members warn him off, but he can't get her out of his mind.

There isn't much that scares Josie Green. She can parachute in to a forest fire and supervise a crew without missing a beat.

But she doesn't trust her own instincts when it comes to the new guy. She has to jump with him in order to see if he's got the stuff to join the hotshot team of firefighters.

Out of all the men in the camp, why is she drawn to *him*?

Smokejumpers work in extreme conditions. Their job combines skydiving and firefighting. They jump from airplanes and land near intense wildfires in areas not accessible by road. Once they've landed, they must fight fires spread over hundreds of acres to protect life, property, and wildlife habitat.

RENEE HART

SLOW BURN IN THE WILDERNESS

Chapter One

Trevor dropped his gear bag at the edge of the camp and took a quick look around at the set-up. He was used to rough accommodations, but this place appeared to be hacked out of the thick forest with a bush knife. Spotting a couple of guys going over their gear next to a small tent, he asked the whereabouts of the crew chief. The two men barely looked up from their task as one of them mumbled something about the supply tent and pointed over his shoulder. Trevor could see a corner of canvas from his position so he headed in that direction.

"You're looking for Jo," one of the men called after him, and Trevor tensed as he heard both men snicker.

He didn't know these guys yet so there was no point in getting riled, he reminded himself. They weren't trying to start anything. Troublemakers didn't last long in this job. Seeing a guy sitting at a makeshift table shoveling beans into his mouth, Trevor headed his way. A slight movement off to one side drew his eye and he found himself looking at a wisp of a girl with auburn hair pulled back into a short ponytail. She was busy juggling a clipboard as she counted her way through a pile of foodstuffs.

Carefully averting his eyes, he made a beeline for the man eating beans.

"Trevor Morris reporting for duty," he said quietly as the man continued to eat.

When he got no response, he repeated the phrase a bit louder. The man ignored him for several more bites before grunting and waving his fork in the direction of the woman. Trevor turned to look in her direction and caught sight of the other two men standing off and watching him. He couldn't help but notice the big grins on their faces. His face turned red as he looked around the clearing for the crew boss.

"I'm Jo, as in Josie," the woman said without turning around, "and never mind those two. They play that stupid joke on every new person that walks in here. Idiots!"

The last word was directed towards the other two guys as they melted off into the woods still grinning like fools. Trevor stood there feeling like an idiot himself. He didn't like being the butt of anyone's joke. Taking a couple of deep breaths to quiet his personal demons, he pulled out his paperwork and waited for her to finish.

"We won't starve," she said, "but someone is going to catch it for sending all this tuna. It's not the kind packed in water."

Trevor didn't know why that mattered so he stayed silent as she took his papers and looked them over.

"Looks like everything's in order so I'll get you on

the jump roster for tomorrow," Jo said. "You can get yourself set up and get your gear in order with Brian here, when he's done stuffing his face."

She turned back to her clipboard leaving Trevor to take care of himself. He headed back for his bag hoping to catch a little shut-eye while it was quiet. The trip out here to the Alaskan Bush hadn't given him much time in the way of real sleep.

He stopped on his way out to check the status board and the map. The main fire had grown a lot bigger since he'd left Boise to come up here. This crew was trying to stay ahead of all the little fires being spawned by the big one. The crazy winds blowing through and around the mountains could carry a spark for miles before dropping it. The job of a smoke jumper sometimes felt like chasing fireflies.

***

Trevor woke up from a deep sleep to the sound of nearby laughter. He figured some more of the crew had arrived and it was time for him to get up. As he headed for the main tent, the smell of food reminded him that he'd been neglecting his stomach. It was time to get something to eat or he was going to be chewing on granola bars all night. He was surprised to see a big pot of something that smelled like chili bubbling on top of a camp stove. Everything he'd eaten in the last couple of weeks was wrapped in plastic and usually cold. This was going to be a treat for him. Grabbing a couple of bowls, he filled them to the brim and looked around for a seat.

Much to his surprise, he saw Jo sitting over at a corner table alone and she appeared to be waving at him. He headed her way thinking he would see what she wanted and maybe grab a seat at her table. Two steps away, a large man intercepted his course and sat down at the seat across from Jo. Trevor tried to change his aim for the seat next to her when an even bigger guy elbowed past him and sat next to her. No one at the table looked at him so he made a quick right and sat at another table.

"You didn't really think you were going to make that play, didja Rookie?" one of the men sitting at the table asked quietly.

"Yeah, what were you thinking?" another guy said as he snickered into his bowl. "You might want to slow down and learn about the other players before you jump into that game."

Trevor was embarrassed by what they apparently thought and tried to explain himself.

"I thought she was waving at me," he said lamely.

"She was. You were standing in front of the wind sock and she's watching for a wind shift," the first man said. "If this turns into a real blow, we're going to have to break camp and make a quick move."

Trevor turned around to check out the view

behind him and could see the man was right. He'd been standing right in her line of sight and she was just trying to get him to move. Having embarrassed himself twice in the same day in front of her, Trevor leaned over and started shoveling food into his mouth. The food was tasteless as he choked it down, more out of necessity than hunger. He'd already lost his appetite.

***

Josie fought to keep her mind off the new guy as she went over the duty roster for the third time, still not seeing the names. She was surprised as jumpers came and went all the time with most of them passing through without making much of an impression on her. This guy was ringing bells in her head from every dark corner. She wasn't looking forward to the next morning. It was her responsibility to make the first few jumps partnered up with him.

Josie's evaluation would be the basis of whether or not he would be accepted as a part of their hotshot team. They only took the best of the best because of the standards her father had set at the beginning. For the first time, Josie doubted her ability to give the guy a fair shake. Every instinct inside of her was screaming a warning that he was somehow about to change everything for all of them and Josie didn't like change. She briefly considered asking her brother to take her place. Shoving the clipboard away in frustration, Josie climbed into her sleeping bag and forced herself to blank out. Her gentle snores soon filled her little tent.

***

Morning came with little fanfare in the Land of the Midnight Sun. In the middle of June night simply didn't come in any real sense of the word as the sun merely slipped below the horizon for a brief moment in time. Trevor knew he'd slept because he woke up, but the strain of traveling on a shoe string budget had left him more than tired. He wondered if a morning was in his near future that didn't involve some kind of struggle to shake off the desire for real sleep.

He'd hitchhiked his way across Canada with only the burning need to get Boise behind him and carry on with his life. The trip was a blur of kindly souls in cars, trucks, RV's, and the occasional logging truck. His best ride came when he met up with a logger heading north out of some little town. The guy was pretty sick and when he learned that Trevor was able to take a turn at the wheel, he crawled in the back and went to sleep. Struggling with his own demons, Trevor drove nearly non-stop until the gas ran out and he had to wake the guy up. The logger wasn't too pleased to find himself a hundred miles beyond his destination.

A deep growl from his stomach reminded him that last night's chili still wasn't sitting too well and he needed to get his tail in gear. The camp was silent with a few snores coming to remind him that he wasn't alone out here in the wilderness. Not being one to wear a watch, he wondered at the time. It seemed late with the sun already high above the trees, but Alaska had a way of stretching time outside the perception of normal. It took some getting used to, he'd been told on the way up.

Coming around the corner of the main tent, he spotted Brian with a rifle slung across his back and a bowl of last night's chili in his hand. He gave Trevor a friendly nod, but didn't pause as he shoveled beans into his mouth. Trevor guessed he'd pulled bear watch last night while the rest of them slept.

The black bears found camp life irresistible here in the Alaskan wilderness. He was glad the grizzlies, didn't share that attitude. This year the state seemed to be overrun with bears and the brown bears had the most formidable reputation with their more aggressive nature. Of course, any bear encounter out here in the wild had a potential to go bad for any human encroaching in their territory. Trevor had heard plenty of stories over the years. He didn't want to be one of those tales no matter how it turned out in the end.

Ignoring the chili, he dug around in the supplies in search of something more like breakfast and came up with some canned fruit and granola. Trying to appear friendly, he went over and sat down next to Brian. The two of them sat there for several minutes, focused on their food.

When Brian was done eating, he pointed out some of the standard features of the camp and gave Trevor a brief rundown on the status of the fire they were fighting.

"The fire's a gobbler and it's running up and down these ridges with the wind pushing it in just about every direction," he said. "Every time we think we've gotten ahead of it, the beast finds a way to slip around us through some hidden ravine or crevice. This one's got a mind of its own."

"How many crews are working this?" Trevor asked quietly.

"Not sure. The last I heard was two, but the call's been out for a third since last week," Brian answered. "There's no one available or no money or some stupid thing like that. We've got eight teams out in the tundra from here."

Neither of the men noticed as Josie came around the corner of the tent. She stopped at the sight of Trevor and took a deep breath. He wasn't the first person she was hoping to see this morning. Steeling herself, she slipped up behind the two men and tapped Brian on the shoulder.

"Brian! If you weren't one of the best smoke jumpers on this team, I'd have to fire you for being one of the worst bear guards," she said sharply. "If I was a bear, I'd of had the jump on both of you!"

"If you were a bear, you wouldn't be smelling all nice and clean like somebody wearing perfume," Brian grinned at her.

"I'm not wearing perfume," Josie retorted. "Some fool decided to wash my clothes with some fancy smelling soap that's all. You know me better than that."

"Bottom line is I smelled you coming long before you tapped my shoulder and that's what makes me a better bear guard than anybody else. Bears stink worse than a wet dog."

"True, but you can't always count on being downwind of them," Josie grinned good-naturedly and went in search of her own sustenance.

Trevor realized this was an old argument rehashed more out of routine than any lapse on Brian's part and relaxed a bit. He'd gone tight as a steel drum at the first sound of her voice. Most women didn't affect him like she did, and he couldn't put his finger on any particular reason for the tension he felt around her. He wasn't used to seeing a lot of women on the hotshot crews, but there were a few working out of and around Boise. They got treated the same as everyone else and once they'd completed training and proved they could do the job, most of the guys just considered them part of the team. He'd never thought of himself as having anything in particular against female smoke jumpers.

"Hey, Rookie! You're jumping with me today," Josie called back over her shoulder.

Trevor flinched.

"I'm not a rookie," he said quietly, mostly to himself.

"Everyone's a rookie here until they've passed muster with Josie," one of the big guys from last night said as he came around the corner.

"We don't have any mustard," Brian said grimly, "or ketchup or relish. Just these nasty canned hot dogs. We don't even have any buns."

Ignoring the complaint, the big guy came over to Trevor and stuck out his hand.

"Mitch Green. I see you've already met my daughter. Don't be fooled by the tough exterior. She's a sweetheart under all that soot."

Mitch laughed as if he'd just said the funniest thing on earth as Josie glared at him from the other side of the tent. For whatever reason, she didn't want anyone pointing anything out about her to the new guy. *Let him make his own decisions about me*, she railed to herself.

"And this is my son, Jake," Mitch continued as Jake came around the corner trying to rub the sleep from his eyes.

"What are you all doing up so early?" he grumbled. "It's only four in the morning!"

Trevor's mouth dropped open in surprise. He thought it must be past nine at least.

"How's Joe Davis doing?" Mitch directed his question at Trevor.

"Uh, he was fine when I last saw him," Trevor replied. "You a friend of his?"

"Sure thing. Joe and I were buddies in the Army. He used to tell everyone that Josie here was named after him. Used to make my wife so mad. Haven't seen or heard from him in more than ten years until he contacted me to recommend you."

The tent went quiet at the mention of Josie's mother as the three of them still carried their own measure of guilt for not being there when she passed away suddenly. None of them even knew she was sick because she kept it from them, and then she was gone. Brian picked up his trash and made a quick exit in search of a bush. Trevor froze as he considered finding someplace else to be by himself. This was clearly family talk and he wasn't family.

Josie was the first to break the silence.

"Our ride will be here within the next couple of hours," she said. "Be ready to go."

No one responded as she made a hasty departure.

"The answer to your question is yes," Jake said when she was out of sight.

"My question?" Trevor said hesitantly.

"Yeah, your question. Is she always this bossy? The answer is yes."

Father and son laughed heartily as Trevor decided it was best to err on the side of caution and not join in with them. He might not be welcome. After all, he wasn't family or even part of the crew yet until Josie had the final word on him. *That doesn't sit real well with me*, he thought to himself.

Chapter Two

Trevor checked over his gear bag one more time before heading over to the air strip. The camp was located off to one side of the rough clearing and a tall mountain range ran along the northern edge of the valley.

There wasn't much to distinguish this place from a lot of other wilderness areas he'd fought fires in over the last ten years. Plenty of trees, brush, and ground fuel to keep a wildfire burning for months and enough lightning strikes to start one at any time of the day or night. He stopped and took a long look at the wide column of smoke clearly visible to the west. The fire wasn't taking a day off.

The two jokesters he'd run into yesterday were already at the pick-up spot working on the tool drops. The teams would take off first, Trevor knew, and the planes would bring in any heavier equipment needed in the field later. They called out a hearty welcome when he came into sight and offered up teasing apologies for yesterday's prank. He took it all in stride.

"So I hear you're out of Boise," Dennis said as he loaded up some heavy boxes into the sling.

Trevor simply nodded.

"What brings you up to Alaska?" he asked. "Not enough fires in Idaho this year?"

Trevor didn't answer as this was the one question he was hoping would never come up. He was happy in Boise until... He knew for him, there was no going back.

Fortunately, the Green team appeared in the clearing at that moment giving him room to ignore the curious looks coming his way from his two crew mates. Trevor knew he'd have to give some kind of answer eventually but he would do his best to avoid that moment for as long as possible. Nothing he could say would ever erase the pain of what happened back in Boise.

***

Josie felt a strange flutter in her chest as she spied Trevor across the field. She actually looked down at the front of her jumpsuit as if something had reached out and touched her there. The distraction caused her to stumble over a tuft of grass and Jake reached out to steady her. She brushed away his touch.

"The plan for today is to evaluate our fire breaks along the northern edge and see if they're holding," Josie said loudly as the others gathered around. "There are four teams out there already and if possible, I'd like to give a couple of teams a break. We'll reassess the situation once we're out in the field."

Everyone nodded in agreement and turned at the sound of the plane heading their way. No one noticed Mitch watching his daughter carefully. He was curious at the tense sound in her voice as she addressed the crew. It wasn't like her to get so riled up over anything, yet she was clearly on edge this morning. He resolved to keep a close eye on her today as she worked with the new guy. Something was amiss.

The plane landed on the rough ground with more than a few bounces and taxied their way. The crew quickly gathered all of their personal gear and loaded up. It was a short flight to their drop zone and no one missed the fact that it was getting shorter every week. Soon it would be time to consider relocating the camp if this fire kept jumping the breaks they were building around it.

"I'll go first," Josie said to Trevor, "and you're on my heels. The drop zone is pretty well-established at this point. There shouldn't be any confusion about where to land."

Trevor nodded and sat next to her, looking out the window. The fumes of plane exhaust mixed with smoke was tinged with another smell that tickled his nostrils. As his keen nose fixated on the scent, he realized he was smelling her and he blushed. She caught the flush on his face and wondered if he was feeling okay. As the spotter called out 3,000 feet, there was no time to ask. It was time to go.

Josie slipped from the open doorway and into the roar of rushing wind. Trevor made his count and followed her. As his chute opened, the stomach churning rush towards the ground ended with a quick jerk across his chest and the only sound came from the parasail rattling his lines. He looked around for his partner. Josie was 300 yards off to his left and already turning to head for their target. He followed her lead not bothering to spot the landing for himself. He figured she knew where they were going.

A sudden gust of wind pulled him off course and he lost sight of her when a cloud of smoke blew in his direction. Cursing himself for not sighting the landing zone, he looked around frantically for a clue as the ground blurred beneath him. Realizing he was out of time, he gave up on the zone and looked for a safe landing spot. He knew he couldn't be that far off course, but he'd just made a rookie's error. This wasn't the way he wanted to start.

Hitting the ground in some heavy brush, he started to unbuckle his chute when a heavy grunt came from his right. He turned in that direction and found himself looking right into the eyes of a very large grizzly. The bear looked almost as surprised as he was and they stared at each other without moving. Josie's voice came to him from the left.

"Whatever you do," she said in a monotone voice, "don't run. It's best if you talk to him in a quiet voice."

Trevor tried to swallow and couldn't find enough spit for that. He wasn't sure how he was going to be able to speak and running was out of the question with his chute still engaged and his legs tangled in brush. He stood there frozen trying to remember anything he'd learned in bear training that might help. Nothing came to mind.

Josie continued talking in a quiet voice but neither of them had a chance if the bear decided they were a threat. The seconds ticked by as the bear grunted and began to swing his head back and forth between them. Trevor realized he was holding his breath.

A sudden gust of wind caught hold of Trevor's chute, filling it full of air and ballooning it upwards. It rose over his head like a giant cape towering over all of them. The bear took one look and made a quick decision to retreat from the threatening sight of the large creature confronting him.

Trevor saw the bear start to move just as his chute flipped over and came down on top of him. He was convinced he was about to become a Kevlar-wrapped bear snack and let out a roar in self-defense. The bear never looked back and as Trevor braced himself for the attack, he suddenly realized Josie was laughing her head off. He struggled to find the edge of his chute as adrenaline fueled his confusion. He had no idea what was so funny right then.

When his face appeared under the leading edge, Josie stopped laughing and pointed in the direction of the bear. His backside was barely visible as he made a beeline for safety. The bear was clearly in no mood for company that day.

"Smooth move, Rookie," Josie called to him. "I'm not sure hiding under your chute would make it into the bear safety handbook, but you managed to make it look practical."

Trevor cast her an annoyed look and wrestled with his chute trying to reestablish some semblance of control. She busied herself with her own gear to give him some time to calm down. This wasn't the time to bust his chops about missing the landing zone. She figured the bear would give him plenty to think about for now.

The two of them joined the other teams and Trevor got busy with the area assigned to him while Josie went off to inspect the fire's progress. He relished settling himself into the familiar routines of digging trenches, clearing brush and cutting down trees. This was the job he was trained to do and he lost himself in the smoke and the sweat. There was no room for bad memories in the field. He was surprised when Josie came up and told him it was time for a break.

"There's a supply drop heading our way," she said as she pointed out the drop zone. "We'll all meet up there and have something to eat."

Grabbing up his tools, Trevor hurried to join the others. His water bottle was empty and his stomach was dancing with its own internal needs. As the crew gathered, Mitch took charge of the introductions. A couple of the guys looked at him curiously but it was clear to all of them that Trevor knew his way around a fire. He'd worked as hard as any of them.

"So, Trevor," one of the guys called out, "I hear you run off that grizzly this morning. That beast's been dogging us for the last couple of days. We thought the fire had chased all the big animals away, but apparently this one didn't want to go."

Trevor tensed as he searched for any sign the guy was mocking him and took a quick look in Josie's direction. She was carefully avoiding his gaze, but he could tell she was listening intently. He decided some humor might help defer any other questions.

"One of us had to run," Trevor said, "and he was the only one in a position to do so with me up to my rear in brush. I was real happy to see his backside... once I got my chute off my head."

His comments brought a laugh from the others and the moment passed. Trevor saw Josie cast a quick glance in his direction along with what he hoped was a look of approval. She turned away real quick to hide the rest of her feelings.

***

The rest of the day passed in a smoky haze as the winds shifted late in the afternoon, forcing the crew to redirect their efforts. Trevor found himself working near Mitch and Jake on a line of fire trying to break through their ranks. They'd cut down several small spruce trees and were using the tops to beat out the little tongues of flame licking up the sparse grass. The three of them worked furiously for nearly an hour until they gained the upper hand and beat the fire back.

Trevor realized Mitch was looking pretty worn and went over to check on him. He was surprised when Jake stepped in front of him redirecting Trevor to go over and help another team. As he turned for a quick look back, he saw Jake walking away from the fire with his father. A sweeping look of the area showed him Josie watching from the far side with a worried look on her face. He knew the signs and realized that Mitch's days as a smoke jumper were numbered. It was clear his son and daughter knew it too.

That evening Josie assigned three teams to stay and watch the line and three teams to head back to camp. Trevor was surprised to be sent back before he realized it was mainly due to him being paired up with her. She had responsibilities on both sides that needed her attention. As everyone headed off to take a break, she reminded him that the two of them would be jumping again in the morning. He barely shrugged an acknowledgment before disappearing in the direction of his tent. Mitch watched him walk away until he was out of sight.

"I'm thinking there's a bit of an attitude problem," Josie said sharply to her father. "Is there something about Boise I need to know about?"

"If there's something about Boise Trevor wants you to know, he'll tell you himself," Mitch stated firmly. "The one thing I can tell you is that he didn't leave Boise because he did something wrong. He left because he did something so right it scared everyone else. That's not something you can hold against a man."

With those words, Mitch turned on his heel and headed off. Josie stood there with her mouth hanging open in surprise. It wasn't like her father to disagree with her, much less come back with something that sounded like a defense of the other guy. His words left her feeling more confused than ever as she wondered what happened back in Boise that had earned her father's respect. There was no use asking any more questions. The story would come when the time was right and not a minute sooner.

***

Back at the camp Trevor took the short hike over to a nearby slough Brian had pointed out to him. The water was cold and brown, reminding him of iced tea. A few of the other guys were already splashing about and making plenty of noise. He was quick to join them as the sweat and smoke of the day left him gritty and smelly. It was a delight to find the brown water left him feeling as clean as if he'd taken a proper bath with soap. The noisy group headed back to camp in search of sustenance, fully revived by their short outing.

Trevor relaxed in the midst of the familiar chatter of fellow fire fighters. It had been a while since he'd been able to let go and just hang out. It felt good. The feeling lasted until they reached the main tent and he spotted Josie watching him. In an instant, his guarded look was back in place and tension took hold of him. *I don't know what it is about her, but she's getting under my skin,* he thought to himself in frustration. *The woman always seems to be looking for me to do something wrong.* He grabbed some food and sat down as far away from her as possible in the small area.

Josie pretended not to notice, but her father saw everything as he carefully noted the way they were acting. Suddenly, Mitch smiled to himself as he recognized the signs and put them together. *I've waited a very long time for something like this to happen and the timing couldn't be better,* he

SLOW BURN IN THE WILDERNESS

thought, still grinning like a fool. Josie looked at him curiously but being busy with her own thoughts, she didn't ask.

***

The next morning, Trevor woke up early again and headed off to find breakfast. The camp was just beginning to stir and someone Trevor didn't know was standing bear guard at the main tent. The two of them nodded at each other.

"Seen any bears around here?" Trevor asked as he gathered some food for himself.

"No, but that don't mean they're not around. Bears can be pretty sneaky. I've heard of fellas walking right by them in the woods and never seeing a thing until the bear'd snuck up behind them and jumped 'em."

"Does that happen a lot?" Trevor asked cautiously.

"Not really, but I always figured once would be enough for anyone."

The guy laughed as if he'd just told a really funny joke, but Trevor didn't join in. He wasn't sure how he felt about bears after yesterday. It would be okay with him if he never saw another one in the wild. He might not be so lucky next time.

As he was heading for a table, he caught sight of Jake and Josie. He could tell they were in the midst of a heated discussion as both of them looked upset. Their hushed tones made it clear this was a private matter but Trevor was drawn to move close enough to overhear them. He felt guilty about spying and tried to make some noise to alert them of his presence. Both of them were caught up in their conversation and didn't hear him.

"I'm telling you, Josie," Jake said heatedly. "This isn't going to last much longer. We can't keep pretending that nothing is happening here."

"You're wrong! You're always looking for something to worry about and I'm not going to be pushed into making the wrong decision," Josie retorted just as heatedly.

"We made a pact! You. Me. And Dad. We all agreed on this before you and I came on board," Jake said in a threatening voice. "If you don't keep your end of it, you know he won't come out either and it'll be on your head!"

Josie stared at her brother defiantly, unwilling to admit he might be right. *He has to be wrong. He just has to be,* she thought to herself before turning away and stomping off towards her tent. Jake sighed and turned towards the mess tent. He froze when he saw Trevor had watched their little family drama. His face tensed with anger towards this outsider for a moment as he started towards him.

"Most people around here know how to mind their own business," Jake said sharply as he pushed

SLOW BURN IN THE WILDERNESS

past Trevor, nearly knocking him over.

"Sorry" was all that came out as Jake disappeared on the far side of the tent.

Trevor's face was red while his mind raced with questions. He didn't know what was going on with the Green's but things clearly weren't working out as expected. Grabbing some extra food, he decided not to wait around the mess tent. It might be better to head over to the airstrip and help with some of the loading. He was sure to find someone doing something over there to take his mind off things he didn't understand.

As he came into the clearing, the one person he'd hoped not to see was staring at him as he approached. Jake wasn't around so Trevor could only hope Josie didn't know he'd been listening to their argument. He forced himself to act natural though his heart was pounding inside his chest. Pulling out a couple of granola bars, he offered her one. He was actually surprised when she took it with a murmur of thanks and began chewing on it noisily. He waited until she was done and offered her the second one in his pocket. She took that one too.

"I take it breakfast wasn't on your list of things to do this morning," he said as he watched her eat.

"I forgot," she mumbled around a mouthful of granola. "The chopper's on the way and I need to get these containers packed up and sent off before we head out to the fire or we won't be getting any supplies this evening."

"I'll help," Trevor said as he turned to the task and got right to work.

The two cargo nets were loaded and ready to go when they heard the chopper heading their way. They both turned and watched its approach, silhouetted by the morning sun's rays. It was a perfect setting for a movie scene. As the chopper slowly let down the line, Josie grabbed it with the hook and Trevor helped her attach the first load. The spotter leaning out the door watched them until she gave an all clear for the chopper to lift the line for the second cargo net to be attached.

Trevor wasn't sure what happened next as everything went crazy in a heartbeat. A strong gust of wind broadsided the chopper causing the line to drag as Josie was attaching the second cargo net. She got tangled in the net and as the load lifted it pulled her up off the ground. The spotter couldn't see her from his side and gave an all clear signal as the pilot fought to steady the chopper. The helicopter rose quickly to avoid running the load into the nearby trees.

Trevor watched in horror as Josie dangled loosely by one arm below the cargo net. He saw the radio slip from her grasp as he began waving his arms frantically to get the spotter's attention. It was clear no one was looking at him and no one on the chopper could see Josie hanging below them. Trevor ran for the radio as the chopper rose higher in the air. He stopped in amazement as she pulled off a move worthy of any circus acrobat and flipped her legs up to wrap them in the net. Grabbing the radio, he was relieved to see that Josie had somehow managed to pull herself up on top of the load and was sitting there comfortably watching the ground recede below her. He yelled the situation into the radio with a long stream of nearly incoherent words.

The spotter leaned out the door and looked down in surprise. It took less than five minutes to get Josie back on the ground unharmed. Trevor ran over and grabbed her by the arms trying to see that she was okay. She was laughing as she pushed him away a bit roughly.

"Stop it! I'm all right," Josie exclaimed, still laughing.

She took the radio from him and gave the pilot an all-clear. The chopper wasted no time in heading off with a wave. Trevor stood there watching her with a mixture of anger, fear, and something he couldn't explain on his face. She stared back at him defiantly.

"If you tell anyone about this," she stated firmly, "I'll tell everyone what really happened with that bear yesterday and how you missed the landing spot."

Trevor's eyebrows went up in surprise.

"You just did this crazy stunt, and you're trying to blackmail me," he exclaimed.

The two of them broke off their conversation as a couple of the other guys stepped into the clearing. They took one look at Trevor and Josie staring at each other with red faces and pretended they'd forgotten something back at camp.

"I mean it," Josie warned, but Trevor could see the laughter still dancing at the corners of her mouth.

He was suddenly overwhelmed with the urge to grab her arms again and kiss her soundly in retaliation for her threats. Even as the thought came, he knew retaliation wasn't the real reason and he quickly turned away. *This woman has me tied up with more knots than a cargo net and I'm not ready for any more complications in my life,* he thought in frustration. Grabbing his gear bag, he headed back to camp for more granola bars.

Still fuming, he stomped through the brush not watching where he was going. The sound of voices caught his attention and he looked up to find Jake and Mitch coming towards him. Inwardly, he groaned as this little camp just wasn't big enough for all of the drama surrounding him. He squared his shoulders expecting another rebuke from Jake about his earlier indiscretion.

When they both saw him, Jake looked at him coldly in sharp contrast to Mitch, who greeted him

SLOW BURN IN THE WILDERNESS

warmly. Trevor mumbled a hasty good morning and acted as if he was in a hurry to get past them. They parted to let him go by and Trevor was sure Jake gave him as little room as possible to force him to squeeze between their larger bodies. As if he wasn't feeling small enough already, he took the insult as his due for eavesdropping earlier and let it go. He didn't want to end up on the wrong side of anyone. If he was going to stay on as a smoke jumper, he needed to earn his position on this hotshot crew.

SLOW BURN IN THE WILDERNESS

Chapter Three

The next few days came and went without incident as the crew gained some ground on the fire and the camp started to feel a bit more relaxed. One morning, Trevor woke up to the sound of a plane landing too early to be shuttling jumpers to the fire break. He got up and headed for the mess tent more out of hunger than curiosity. Finding Brian with his face in a bowl of beans, he called out a hearty good morning, receiving the usual grunt from the big guy.

Trevor wandered over to the status board and was surprised to find he'd been reassigned to jump with Jake. He quickly scanned the names on the rest of the teams. Josie and Mitch weren't on the list of teams going out that day.

Since his little indiscretion of eavesdropping hadn't come up again, Trevor was pretty sure Jake hadn't mentioned it to Josie. She'd treated him in her usual bossy manner on their last few jumps. Jake wasn't acting too friendly towards him, but he wasn't showing any real hostility either. Trevor could only hope that would continue as they worked together. He really respected the way Jake looked out for his father. It was a pretty good bet the conversation he'd overheard was related to Mitch's condition. It was clear to him the older man was struggling. He just didn't know how, and was in no position to be asking any questions.

Working his way through some canned fruit and instant oatmeal, Trevor kept one ear to the ground and soon learned that Mitch and Josie had flown out early that morning. With Jake in charge, the guys headed for the airstrip to work on widening their firebreak. The winds had dropped enough in the last few days to give them time to clear out a significant amount of brush to the north. At their current pace, the fire would be contained within a couple of weeks and it would be time for this team to move on to another part of the state. The hot, dry summer was keeping every hotshot crew on their toes as they worked hard to protect life, property, and wildlife habitat. It was a job all of them felt mattered and they put their hearts into it.

Trevor and Jake were the last team to jump when they reached the landing zone. The familiar rush of the wind in his face gave Trevor the usual rush of adrenaline. He grinned widely as the chute slowed his descent, giving him time to take a look around. This was the best part of his day. Catching sight of Jake's face, he saw an answering grin as the two of them took an extra turn around the zone before touching down.

As they made their way across the black, Jake gave Trevor a long, hard look.

"How long have you been a jumper?" Jake asked suddenly.

"I went right into training the day after I hit eighteen. I would have been there the same day, but my birthday was on Sunday so I had to wait a day," Trevor said with a grin.

"Anyone else in your family a jumper?"

Trevor looked down before he answered. This wasn't a part of his life he cared to share with just anyone. Swallowing hard, he said quietly, "I don't have any other family. Grew up in foster homes. Never learned anything about where I came from or how I came to be."

Jake was silent for a while before he responded, "Tough way to grow up."

The two men reached the others without continuing the conversation.

***

Josie watched her father climb out of the plane in Anchorage as he tried to hide his pain from her. She was surprised last evening after supper when he asked her to accompany him to town. He usually handled the in-town stuff on his own, leaving her in charge. Hoping to gather the evidence she needed to prove her brother wrong, she quickly agreed and put together the duty rosters for Jake. He hated having to do any kind of paperwork. If it was left up to him, everyone would figure out on their own what they wanted to do and just go do it. He figured they were all adults anyway. Her brother never pretended to anyone that he ever wanted to be in charge of anything.

"I've got an appointment at ten," Mitch said as they dropped off their stuff. "I'll meet you for lunch. We don't have a lot to do on this trip so I thought you might like to spend some time shopping."

Josie's eyebrows shot up in surprise. Shopping was never on her list of fun things to do and her dad knew that.

"I think I'd rather spend my time in the bathtub," she said staring at him suspiciously.

He ducked her stare and headed for the door.

"I was just hoping to have lunch with my beautiful daughter," he said with a laugh as he quickly slipped out the door. "And I'd like to see her in something other than yellow Kevlar for a change."

The last bit was shouted in self-defense through the closed door. As he expected, a loud thud followed his words, indicating she'd thrown something as her response. He chuckled to himself as he walked away. She was clearly a chip off the old block, he mused to himself.

The thought of being an *old block* reminded him of the purpose of this visit. He steeled himself for bad news as he headed for the doctor's office. There was no way to avoid the fact that age was catching up to him. He'd lived too long and too hard on the edge of danger and no doctor was going to be able to change that. If he wanted to live long enough to dangle grandchildren on his knees, he was going to have to give up the life he had for a gentler one. The real problem was going to be convincing Josie to face the same reality. It was clear she was in denial on his account. He knew Jake was already on his side.

***

Tossing herself face down on the bed, Josie enjoyed the soft comfort of a real mattress as she thought about her father's words. Her mother had been the perfect china doll and she made looking beautiful into an art form. As soon as she could chose her own clothes, Josie threw herself into being a tomboy with reckless abandon and rejected her mother's efforts to teach her anything about being feminine. After years of wearing jeans and t-shirts, she didn't own a single dress.

Once her mother had passed, Josie closed her mind to that side of life. It didn't fit into the hobo existence she shared with her father and brother as a smoke jumper. The three of them were either traveling or camping. There was no place for a fancy wardrobe of girlie clothes. She was surprised to find her father's suggestion struck an answering chord somewhere deep inside of her. Maybe showing up for lunch in something...pretty would make her father happy. She pushed away the thought tickling at the back of her mind of someone else she'd like to impress and headed off to give shopping a try. It was times like these when her mother's absence became more real.

Spotting a likely store with dresses in the window, Josie shook off the tension in her neck and shoulders. A dress was out of the question as it would require shoes and possibly more than she was willing to risk. She cast a critical eye at the racks, hoping something would jump out at her. The sales clerk watched her carefully and then turned away to assist another customer. Feeling overwhelmed and out of place, Josie chose that moment to retreat and headed for the door. *I would have done better if the store was on fire and I had to make the choice of what to let burn and what to save,* she thought to herself in frustration as she nearly ran out of the store.

She headed back to the hotel hoping to slip into the tub before lunchtime came and she had to face her father again. Her defeat burned inside of her. She filled the tub with the hottest water she could stand and slipped into the soothing warmth. Losing herself in the comfort, she was surprised to hear the door open.

"Josie," came Mitch's voice much to her relief.

"I'm in the tub," she called back, hurrying to get out and see why he was back so soon.

"I bought you something," her dad called out. "I'm going down to the coffee shop. I'll see you when you get done."

Curious about what her father had bought, Josie waited until she heard the door close before coming out of the bathroom. A gaudy shopping bag sat in the middle of her bed. Approaching it cautiously, she leaned over to take a peek inside. Pink! Her own father went out and bought her something pink! The very idea was enough to shake her up. Grabbing the edge of the bag, she shook the garment out onto the bed.

At first glance, she could tell it was just a girlie looking blouse. Nothing too fancy but it was definitely at the far edge of her comfort zone. She picked it up by one corner gingerly and shook it out. The soft cloth draped gently from her fingers with a quiet shimmer of elegance. This clearly wasn't some cheap piece of fluff. She searched for a price tag or sales receipt.

Mitch was clever enough to have removed both, leaving her without a clue as to the cost or origin. It was hers to keep. The real question was, did she have the courage to wear it. Even as the thought came, she scoffed. Courage wasn't something she lacked so why did wearing a simple blouse give her any trouble. She'd just put it on right then and there.

Turning her back to the mirror, she began to get

dressed.   Following her usual routine of socks, underwear and jeans, she suddenly remembered her wet hair. It wouldn't do to put the silky blouse on over a wet head. Rubbing her head with a towel, she stared at the unfamiliar garment.

An old memory of her mother played out in her mind. Josie could almost hear her mother's voice.

"Someday you'll grow up and become a beautiful young lady," her mother said, *gently brushing her hair, "and then you'll see things differently."*

"No, I won't," the young girl retorted. *"I'm going to be a smoke jumper like Daddy! I'm never going to be like you."*

Josie remembered the sad look on her mother's face as if it had happened yesterday. She wasn't trying to hurt her mother that day but she had, and the distance between them grew until their relationship was broken beyond repair. Her mother gave up the dream of having a daughter like herself and lived her life at the fringes of their adventurous pursuits.

When Josie and her brother went into smoke jumper training, her mother was left behind at the ranch alone. The three of them went home between fires at first, but other reasons began to keep them away for longer and longer spans of time until the ranch felt more like a stopover place than home. Her mother built a life for herself with friends and hobbies. When she died, the funeral was a sea of unfamiliar faces for Mitch, Jake and Josie. After that, they closed up the house and stopped going back at all. Josie wasn't sure which one of them carried the most guilt, but she suspected she was close behind her father with her load. She didn't want to let her father down the same way she'd hurt her mother.

Giving her hair one final rub, she lifted the blouse gently from the bed and let it slip down her arms. As it settled over her curves, she looked down with awe on her face. The color, the fabric and the fit all worked together to transform her somehow. She turned to the mirror to confirm her first impression. The beautiful young woman staring back from the glass caused a flush to come to her face. She realized in that moment her mother's words from so long ago had finally come true.

***

The fire appeared to have accepted the boundaries allotted to it and the crews turned their efforts to clean-up and maintenance tasks. Everyone knew things could change in a heartbeat with heavy winds, more lightning, or human error coming into play. With the bosses away and Jake in charge, the camp quickly took on a more casual air. Once a week, the chopper brought in a special meal of fresh food and this week's special was steak and baked potatoes.

Brian took over the makeshift grill and demonstrated his culinary skill. Trevor disappeared for a while leaving everyone to wonder but soon came back with a solar oven he'd fashioned from some boxes and tin foil. He mixed up a concoction of granola and canned peaches that baked up into a wonderful peach cobbler. All of the men ate their fill as they enjoyed this brief respite from the hazards of their job.

"Hey Brian," Trevor called across the mess tent, "this is the first time I've seen you eating something besides beans. How's that steak?"

"Steak's good," Brian exclaimed around a mouthful, "cause I cooked it!"

A round of cheers went up from his fellow crewmates as everyone heartily agreed.

"This cobbler's not too bad either," Jake said from across the table. "You're going to have to teach me your technique."

Trevor smiled as he relaxed into the comradery of food and friends. It had been a long time since he'd felt like a part of the team. There was just one thing missing at this point and he couldn't put his finger on it. As he slipped into his sleeping bag later that evening, he realized what it was as he once again felt himself listening for a plane or chopper that would bring Mitch and Josie back to camp. He couldn't remember a time in his life when he actually missed another person. It was a strange feeling.

***

Mitch was on his third cup of coffee as he sat in the diner trying to figure out how to talk to his daughter. He'd never been good with words and his children took after him. Their mother did most of the talking, it seemed, as they were growing up. He was more about doing and while his efforts managed to win him their mother's heart, there was no doubt he'd failed to deserve it. He'd let his job push all of her needs and wants to the back burner every time there was something to do or someplace to go. His final failure was to steal away her daughter into the life of a smoke jumper, leaving her alone at the end. He'd never intended things to go that way but Josie saw him as a hero and he'd done nothing to dispel her worship.

Now he was in the same position and still selfishly wanting his choices to prevail in his children's lives or he would spend his final years alone also. He'd made a foolish pact with them when they joined him as fire fighters, putting his needs first. If they chose to go on without him, he knew his life would slip away with him, rattling around the ranch until he died. His other concern was that if they chose to honor the pact, he'd be stealing some of their best years as fire fighters from them. He was having a hard time convincing himself that he had a right to do such a thing. Even worse, the idea of not being there for Josie if she got herself in trouble, kept him awake at nights. The young woman was fearless and capable, but as her father he still felt responsible for her.

His thoughts were interrupted when the door to the diner opened and Josie came in. His breath caught in his throat as the past and the present blurred before his eyes. He'd been sitting in a coffee shop just like this the first time he'd seen his wife. Some people laugh at the idea of love at first sight, but Mitch never questioned the idea again after that day. He knew she was the only woman that he'd ever seen in that way and nothing would be right until she said yes.

Josie paused in the doorway, her eyes searching for him. As their eyes met, he swallowed the lump in his throat and his vision blurred with sudden tears. Her eyes lit up and she hurried over to join him, suddenly feeling aware of other eyes upon her. Seeing the tears in his eyes, she slipped into the seat next to him and put her hand on his shoulder.

"Are you all right," she asked anxiously. "What did the doctor say?"

Her father wasn't a man given to showing emotion anywhere. It frightened her to see him all

SLOW BURN IN THE WILDERNESS

choked up in public. He turned away trying to gather his scattered thoughts and hide his feelings.

"Sorry. You caught me by surprise that's all," he mumbled. "You look so much like your mother."

Josie looked down at the blouse she was wearing and smoothed her hands down the front of the soft fabric.

"Thank you," was all she could manage as the waitress arrived to take their order.

When the waitress moved on, Mitch looked at Josie, carefully noting her hair gently resting on her shoulders, free from the usual ponytail and the soft blush on her tanned cheeks. He watched her nervously fidget with the silverware as she avoided his gaze.

"Josie," Mitch said quietly.

She looked up at him and forced her hands into her lap.

"It's over for me. I'm done. I've been fighting fires long enough. I need to move on."

Josie started to protest but he held up his hand to silence her.

"Let me finish."

"I know we all agreed we'd leave together but my motivations in making that pact were selfish. I can't hold you or Jake to it, but it's going to tear my heart to pieces to break up the Green team. I've always seen us as staying and leaving together."

Josie stared at the top of the table as she

struggled to see what the future held for the three of them. They'd never talked about the future beyond the next fire. It had always hung out there in the distance without shape or form for her. She was at a complete loss for words as her father watched carefully for any signs of agreement or dissent. He was unprepared for either.

Much to their relief, the waitress returned with their order and the two of them spent the rest of the meal in silence picking at their food. Neither of them made any pretense of acting as if nothing was wrong and the waitress carefully avoided the dark cloud surrounding their table. Finally Mitch paid the tab and they walked outside into the bright sunshine of the Anchorage evening.

Josie reached out and took hold of her father's arm as they walked. He smiled down at her gently as she took note of the slight slump in his shoulders and his careful gait. Taking note of the weary look on his face, she steered them back to the hotel hoping he could get some rest. There was no more point in denying that his age was finally catching up to him. All the signs had been there for her to see if she'd only bothered to look for herself. She almost resented the fact that Jake was the first to see the truth and accept it. She should have been paying more attention, she berated herself.

Leaving her father at his room, she headed for a nearby park and watched children playing at the playground. For the first time, she wondered what it would be like to have children of her own as she took note of the mothers and a few fathers around her keeping close eyes on their little ones. Seeing a little boy with Trevor's dark eyes and thick hair brought him to mind and she wondered if he ever dreamed of being a father.

These unfamiliar thoughts took on a life of their own as she imagined all of the steps involved in becoming a family. It seemed her dreams were ahead of the reality her father had presented to her in the diner. Suddenly, she could see the possibilities of what life could hold for all of them if she was willing to let go of this one. The future would become whatever the three of them wanted to make it, or was there a fourth to be considered in all this. The thought persisted as she headed back to the hotel.

SLOW BURN IN THE WILDERNESS

Chapter Four

The camp was mostly deserted when Josie and her father returned the next day. They slipped back into the familiar routine of checking over gear and supplies without talking. Yesterday hung between them like a giant question mark. As the crew trickled back in from the field, everyone gave their assessment of the areas they'd worked leaving Mitch to determine the current status. He was optimistic this fire was no longer a threat.

When Jake and Trevor returned together, Josie carefully avoided both of them for as long as possible in the small camp. Trevor didn't seem to notice, but Jake was fuming as he wanted a private word with her to get an update on their father. He finally managed to head her off on the way back from the latrine.

"What did the doctor say?" Jake asked her quietly.

"I don't know," Josie said avoiding his eyes.

She could feel him staring at her.

"He didn't tell me," she finally protested as her brother continued to block her way.

"You know he won't be able to pass the next physical," Jake said.

"I know," she said flatly. "He told me...he's done."

"So that's it. What are you going to do?" Jake asked.

"We…I promised," Josie said sadly. "So I'm going to do the right thing. What about you?"

Jake sighed. He lifted his eyes and looked at the nearby mountains, the trees and the sky.

"This is all I know," he finally said. "I'm not sure I can just walk away."

Understanding what her brother said brought the realization that he'd been looking for her to quit and go with their father. It was never in his heart to keep the pact that bound the three of them together. Her anger flared up bright and hot against him. Using all of her strength, she shoved him as hard as she could and turned to run away.

Surprised, Jake fell back and watched her flight silently. He knew her every thought towards him in that moment as only twins can do, and he felt the full weight of her condemnation. His shame wasn't that he loved his work, but more about how he loved his family less. He'd grown up to become his father's son in every way. There was little hope in his heart that she would ever forgive him for this betrayal and he hated himself in that moment for her sake.

She ran blindly towards the airstrip, fighting the tears that threatened to overwhelm her at every step. The trees blurred and the brush snatched at her causing her to stumble. She'd made it to the far end

SLOW BURN IN THE WILDERNESS

of the landing area before a clump of grass threw her off balance and caused her to crash headlong into a pile of weeds and sticks. She lay there panting as she pounded the ground in rage. This wasn't fair!

Hearing the crack of a broken stick behind her, she rolled over, grabbing a rock in one hand and a stick in the other. She was suddenly aware of the danger that lurked out here in the wilderness and the stupidity of being out here alone. It would serve her brother right if a bear ate her, she thought childishly as she looked carefully at her surroundings.

When Trevor stepped out of the nearby trees with a rifle slung over her shoulder, she tensed as her anger flared again. She rose to a fighting stance on one knee.

"Bear patrol," Trevor called to her warily before turning to continue on his way.

He knew she was upset and didn't want her to know he'd followed to make sure she was safe. She watched him go without answering. The thought of being eaten by a bear suddenly didn't seem so appealing. She stood up quietly and followed him back to camp. He carefully gave her no indication that he knew she was behind him, but his ears were attuned to her every step of the way. She headed straight to her tent and disappeared. He stood nearby watching until he was sure she was going to stay put and then headed off in his own direction.

When Jake and Josie didn't show up for supper, Mitch ate alone and turned in early. Jake wasn't in their tent and didn't come in until long after his father had fallen asleep. He spent the rest of that night thinking about nothing in particular. At some point he noticed the wind had shifted to come out of the north. He knew the north winds could change everything for them by morning. If the fire went on the run to the south, they'd be looking at a whole new strategy. There were people living in that direction.

Jake wasn't the only one listening to the wind change. Josie was sitting in the main tent checking the weather patterns. The fire was contained on the southern edge by a river but high winds could easily blow sparks across and start new fires on the other side. The crew working on the south edge wasn't equipped for a prolonged battle. They'd mainly been brought in to do maintenance on the fire break and keep watch. Their location put them directly in the path of the fire if it broke through on the southern edge. She worked through the night gathering every bit of data they needed to meet this new challenge.

The next morning began early as every fire fighter learned early on in their careers to pay attention to the wind. Their lives depended on knowing which way the wind was blowing and the potential of every shift to change everything. They gathered quickly and waited for their assignments. The camp was too far from the southern edge to hike in, forcing them to jump into the narrow gap of black between the fire and the river. Using the data she'd gathered from the spotter planes, Josie assigned teams as fast as Mitch rolled out the new plan of attack. Everything jumped into high gear as the crew scrambled to stay ahead of this new threat. From the look of the sky, it was going to be a very long day for all of them.

When they reassembled at the southern edge, two teams started in with the oil burners and their hand tools to clear a safe zone for the crew. Mitch and Jake headed off towards the west along the river to check the fire break while Josie and Trevor headed east. The rest of the crew cut beaters from nearby spruce trees and started working the leading edges of the fire. The fire break was slowing the progress of the leading edge but the wind was blowing a lot of smoke and ash in their direction.

Trevor tried to keep pace with Josie but she was smaller and quicker through the thick brush. He lost sight of her a couple of times as she ran ahead fueled by adrenaline and her anger still burning hotly inside of her. She'd carefully hid her unsettled state of mind from her father, but her brother knew she was still seething with rage. He'd hoped for a chance to warn Trevor to keep a close eye on her but there'd been no time. The truth was Trevor didn't need a warning as he was able to read the tension gripping her neck and shoulders as worry lines deeply etched her forehead. He knew she wasn't all stressed out about the fire. This was personal.

He caught up with her just as she reached the end of the fire break cut by the other team. The fire was already seeking a path around the eastern end, with fingers of fire reaching towards the river. Josie shouted her report into the radio calling for air assistance as Trevor jumped to put out some stray flare-ups from windblown sparks.

Suddenly an isolated stand of black spruce burst into flames as the fire snuck in under some brush. The nearest tree exploded, sending flaming arrows of broken branches flying in every direction. The two of them burst into action trying to contain this outbreak. They worked for several minutes as they waited for the water drop to arrive.

Trevor stopped to listen for the sound of the plane but the roar of the fire drowned out every sound. He turned to look back down their path of retreat only to find it was gone as a stream of fire raced to the river in a rush of wind.

Josie started to run towards the fire thinking they'd fight their way back to the safe zone where her father and brother waited. Trevor grabbed her arm to stop her.

"We can't make it back that way," he shouted at her over the roar of the fire. "We need to get to the river!"

"The river's too deep and too fast," Josie yelled back. "Without a raft we'll drown in a heartbeat. The river's full of silt and it'll suck us right to the bottom!"

"I can fix that," Trevor said grimly grabbing her by the arm and running towards the river.

Josie shouted their status into the radio hoping someone was listening as Trevor dragged her along. She wanted to be angry at him and reassert herself as the one in charge but a part of her realized it was mainly her fault they'd gone too far from the safe zone to make it back in time. She'd let her anger at Jake drive her forward without thinking about where she was headed and now her team was in trouble.

At the river's edge they stopped and looked in every direction for some way to get across. The muddy brown water swirled and rolled along appearing docile on the surface like many an Alaskan river, but underneath the current boiled and raged unseen. Many a man had drowned by misjudging the force of the water that pulled anything in the current down to the bottom as it filled the person's clothing with the weight of the heavy silt, condemning them to its watery depths.

Josie turned to look back at the fire raging

behind them as Trevor went to work on a stand of poplars with his Pulaski. She ran to help him.

"We can build a small raft and float down past the fire," Trevor shouted as he laid four lengths of the tree together and began to lash his end with his rappelling rope.

Josie saw what he was doing and quickly followed his lead, lashing her own ends together.

"It's too small," she shouted back looking at the small platform barely big enough for them to lay on side by side.

"This will work," Trevor said grimly as he tied it off to a tree and began to ease it into the water.

Josie looked at the contraption doubtfully and turned to look for some other solution. *There's no way I'm getting on that flimsy thing out in that river,* she thought to herself. It wasn't going to matter how good a swimmer she was when her jump suit filled with silt.

Simultaneously, two things happened. The fire reached another stand of black spruce, turning the trees into torches and the raft began to bob up and down gently on top of the river as the current pulled it away from the bank.

Reaching out his hand, Trevor looked into her eyes.

"You have to trust me," he said firmly.

Swallowing hard, Josie took his hand as he helped her lie face down on one side of the raft. He

SLOW BURN IN THE WILDERNESS

quickly laid down next to her, creating a balance against her lighter weight. Cutting the rope holding them to the bank, he shoved off with one leg propelling them towards the middle of the river. Water splashed over the two of them from the force of his kick, but the raft stayed steady in the water.

Trevor rested one arm over her and some of his weight on her partly to balance the raft and partly to shield her from any sparks that might rain down on them from the fire as they raced along, already caught up by the swift current. She rested under him without moving as the river carried them away from the danger and into the unknown. The radio and the rest of their gear lay on the bank, forgotten as the fire lapped at the edges of the water. The two of them were on their own.

***

Mitch determined the firebreak was still holding up on their end and motioned for Jake to head back to the rest of the crew. It didn't take long for them to reach the safety zone where the rest of the crew members worked side by side to maintain the fire break. Joining the others, Mitch took a look around for Josie and Trevor. Catching Brian's eye, he raised an eyebrow in question. The grim look he got in return was sufficient to answer his question and he tried to make radio contact with no luck.

Jake was also watching carefully for his sister's

return, but the heavy smoke blowing past them left no doubt the fire had cut them off. He started in that direction and then turned back to look at his father in frustration. She was more than his sister. She was a fully trained, experienced fire fighter. He had to believe she was doing what needed to be done to survive.

When the pilot confirmed a water drop on the eastern end of the fire break, Mitch asked for a status on his team members. Again there was no response and the crew was forced to retreat to the safety zone as the wind continued to push the fire towards the river. The men hunkered down in the middle of the black, an area burned to ash already, and waited for the fire to go past them. They would fight it from the backside when the river forced it to slow down.

Between the roiling smoke and flames raging around them, the men could see the sky was turning dark with heavy storm clouds. The sound of thunder was lost in the roar of the fire, but the ground rumbled beneath their feet. Occasional flashes of lightning split the sky to the west and the wind picked up blowing ash and sparks all around them. Hope began to rise in the men as a heavy rain would change everything back to their advantage if it came in time. At this point they could only watch and wait for whatever came next.

***

Trevor knew they were out of reach of the fire, but the current was holding them to the center of the river. He had no way of steering the raft and dared not change his position for fear of tipping them off. He watched the bank racing by as he willed it to draw closer.

A sudden scraping sound alerted them to the shallow sandbar that had snagged the raft. They were stranded next to a logjam caught up on a narrow bridge of rocks. The two of them jumped up and scrambled through the mess leaving, the raft to rejoin the river's flow.

"Any ideas on where we are?" Trevor ventured as he looked around at the thick brush all along the bank of the river.

He ducked suddenly as a flash of lightning split the sky right over his head. The answering boom of thunder announced the storm they were about to experience firsthand without shelter.

Josie calmly pulled a map out of her pocket and started working her way along the river with her finger.

"Any ideas on how far we traveled on the raft?" she asked as the wind tried to rip the map from her hands and large drops of rain began to fall around them.

Trevor shook his head no and stood up to look

around again.

"Then I have no idea," Josie said, "but there are some small trapper cabins along this stretch of the river. If we can get to higher ground, we might be able to spot something."

Trevor found a break in the brush and pushed his way through to a narrow path. Another flash of lightning prompted Josie to jump up and follow him. A gust of wind blew a smattering of rain into their faces. They shivered as the cold air chilled their wet clothing. Both of them were already soaked to the skin.

They hadn't traveled very far when the path they were on crossed another wider path. Josie carefully searched both sides of the path for any kind of markers.

"This looks like a trap line," she said. "On one end, there's probably a cabin. On the other....."

"We've just gotta pick the right direction," Trevor grinned back at her.

The two of them stared at their two choices in frustration as the thunder continued to rumble and the rain picked up.

"I say this way," they both shouted at the same time while pointing in opposite directions.

"Okay," they both said, turning to point the other way simultaneously.

The two of them burst out laughing.

"Flip a coin," Trevor suggested with a wide grin.

"Don't have any," Josie quipped back at him.

Searching the ground around them, Trevor found a small round rock with a mark on one side.

"This side we go east," he shouted over the wind and the rain, "the other we go west."

Josie nodded as he tossed the rock into the air. The sudden appearance of a large bull moose blocking the trail to the east caused both of them to lose sight of the rock. They turned as one and started running west. Josie quickly got ahead of Trevor, much to his chagrin as he struggled to keep pace with her. They ran for what seemed to Trevor like hours as Josie continued without a pause, seeming to draw energy from the storm raging around them.

When she stopped suddenly, he was barely able to keep from bowling her over by diverting his momentum around a handy tree. She didn't try to hide her amusement as he crash-landed in a pile of thorny wild roses. He ignored her as he spied the reason for her abrupt halt. The ramshackle cabin in front of them looked as if it had weathered far more storms than they'd ever seen in their lifetimes. They looked around carefully for any sign of inhabitants, either two- or four-legged, but it was clear no one had taken advantage of this as shelter for a long while.

A nearby flash of lightning drove them to the front door that was latched with a sliding bolt.

Flinging the door open, Trevor looked inside as Josie pushed past him to get out of the storm. A quick inventory of the place revealed an old wood stove with a rickety stovepipe, a cot shredded to pieces by squirrels, a pile of sticks in one corner that looked suspiciously like a nest, and some empty shelves.

"It's not a castle, I'm afraid," Trevor said wryly, "but at least it's not raining on us."

Just as he said that a leak burbled through the roof and several drops of water rained down on his head. Josie laughed as he took a step to one side and shrugged.

"Let me rephrase that," he said with a grin, "at least it's not raining on *one* of us."

He bent over to examine the stove.

"Do you think two fire fighters can get a small fire going in this contraption without burning the place down?" he said, eyeing the pile of sticks.

"You bet," Josie said pulling a lighter out of her pocket and flicking it alight, "and I've got just the thing here."

"Hmmm... fire fighter, or would-be arsonist?" Trevor asked as he rattled the stove pipe and listened to the rain of creosote.

Determining a small fire would be safe enough, he gathered the sticks and lit a small pile to check the draft. Soon he had a small blaze going and the cabin began to warm.

"We need to get out of these wet clothes and take inventory of our supplies," Josie said as she began emptying her pockets.

She made a small pile on one shelf as Trevor followed suit on another. The two of them were sneakily eyeing each other's piles. Trevor pulled a granola bar from his pocket and laid it on his shelf.

"What's that?" Josie said turning to look at the door.

Trevor turned to see what she was looking at as she grabbed the granola bar from his shelf.

"Hey! That's mine," he protested as she spun away from him and ripped the packet open with her teeth.

"But you were going to share it with me, right?"

Josie danced and spun around the little cabin trying to keep away as he attempted to grab the food from her.

"Share, yes. Give it all to you? No!"

He caught her around the waist from behind as he heard her noisily chomping on the granola. She wrested away from his grasp and turned with her back to the wall. He advanced on her with a threatening look on his face as she extended half of the granola bar to him. His emotions raged inside of him. He didn't stop until they were nearly nose to nose and the granola bar was between them with her arm against his chest.

Surprising her with his swiftness, he chomped

down on the bar and began chewing on it loudly right in her face. She laughed as bits of granola flew from his mouth and rained down on her. Pushing him away, she made sounds of disgust as she resumed her previous task. The two of them kept their faces carefully turned away as they both struggled to slow their breathing. Neither of them dared to look as their outer clothes were stripped off.

They fashioned a drying rack from the frame of the cot and arranged their clothing in front of the stove to dry. Trevor used a Mylar blanket from his pocket to form a small area of warmth for them. They settled to the floor to take stock of their supplies and wait out the storm raging outside. It didn't take long for their damp under clothes to dry as they studied the small map from Josie's stash.

"There's a small logging road here," she pointed out, "and a fire road over in this area. When the storm passes, we can try to get a better idea of what's closer. There's also a few native fishing villages along the river if you want to go back and build another raft."

Trevor didn't answer and Josie realized he'd fallen asleep leaning against the wall of the cabin. His quiet snores reminded her of just how tired she was feeling. It didn't take her long to add her own little chorus to the symphony of the storm raging around them. They slept until the little fire in the stove went out and the cold started to creep back in to the little cabin. Drawn to each other's warmth, Trevor put his arms around her in the darkness and held her gently. She leaned against him and both of them dreamed of better times.

A bolt of lightning struck a nearby tree jolting them both awake. Confused by the sudden noise, they quickly moved apart in the darkness. Trevor found his lighter and flicked it on to reveal her rubbing the sleep from her eyes.

"I didn't realize how tired I was," she laughed as a big yawn overcame her.

He nodded in agreement as he felt the warm spot where her head had rested against his chest. Trying to hide his jumbled feelings, he stepped outside to relieve himself and check on the storm. It was still raining heavily, but the winds had completely died down. He pretended not to notice her as she came out and took a stance on the other side of the cabin.

"This rain is good," she called as she headed back inside. "This is the break we really needed to beat that fire."

The two of them hurried back inside. As Trevor restarted the fire, Josie settled back against the wall and watched him carefully.

"How'd you become a smoke jumper?" Josie asked, hoping to start a conversation.

"The usual way," Trevor said. "Go to training. Take the tests. Find someone willing to let you on their crew."

"That's not what I meant," Josie grumbled, "and you know that."

"Oh. You meant to ask *why* I became a smoke jumper."

Trevor was quiet as he sorted out his thoughts. He didn't know how much he wanted to tell her but something inside of him was pushing to tell her everything and let the chips fall where they may. If she rejected him because of his past, he wanted to get it over with before he was too far gone to go on living without her. He dared not consider it might already be too late for him.

"I lived near this old airfield in Texas for a while. I would hang out there doing odd jobs for anybody that would let me near their planes. One day a crew of jumpers came in for a wildfire and spent about a month camping there. I started doing errands and stuff for them and they let me hang around. After a month of their company, I never thought of being anything else," Trevor finished with a laugh. "How about you?"

"I'm sure you can figure that out for yourself," Josie began. "My dad was a drill sergeant in the Army and he trained jumpers. When he came out, he went into firefighting, wildfires mostly. He and his buddy Joe, your friend, got recruited to start up a training camp for smoke jumpers. Somewhere in there, he met my mom, Jake and I came into the

SLOW BURN IN THE WILDERNESS

world, and we followed in our father's footsteps."

"So, you wanted to be like your big brother?"

"Actually, he's my little brother. I'm nine minutes older than him."

"You mean, you're twins?!"

Trevor couldn't hide his surprise at this strange twist.

"I thought twins looked alike or something. You two are polar opposites," he exclaimed.

"We're not identical twins. We're fraternal twins and that kind doesn't usually have that much in common beyond a birthdate and a strange kind of bond that only another twin can understand."

Trevor was quiet as he took in this new information.

"What about you?" Josie continued. "Any brothers or sisters?"

"I don't know," Trevor said quietly. "I grew up in foster homes. No one ever told me anything about where I came from or how I got born. Just this one lady when I was little who told me some silly story about being born in a cabbage patch. I figured that explained why I hate cabbage to this day."

It was Josie's turn to sit quietly. She struggled to find the courage to ask the question she'd been dying to ask since they'd first met. *There's no way he'll bring it up if I don't*, she argued with herself.

"What happened to you in Boise?" she asked in barely a whisper, as if that could somehow make the question okay.

Trevor shifted uncomfortably beside her and rubbed the back of his neck. He was surprised to find there was a willingness in him to tell her. It wasn't like he'd done something wrong or had anything to hide. He'd simply done what he had to do. He took a deep breath and held it for several seconds as she waited silently.

"I went into training the day after I turned eighteen," Trevor began. "There was this other guy I hooked up with and we always ended up as partners. Dylan and I did everything together. In a fire, we were like a well-oiled machine. It was like we could read each other's minds sometimes."

Josie nodded and waited for Trevor to go on as he choked back the pain he still felt at losing his best friend. She knew from her brother what it was like to have that kind of relationship with someone.

"We were working a big fire in Washington. Dylan got snagged in this big, old cypress. I was on the ground teasing him. Trying to get his chute free, the branch he was standing on broke. He fell about twenty feet breaking another half dozen branches before his rope caught hold. We just thought he'd broken a couple of ribs."

"He went on medical leave. I stayed to finish out the season and then went looking for him. It was like he'd disappeared. Joe asked me to help out at an off-season training camp for some rookies. I figured Dylan would turn up when he was ready."

Trevor stopped talking and tended the fire as he relived the next part of his story in his mind. Doing the right thing or the wrong thing seemed to depend more on one's perspective than any actual cut and dried formula. There were always people willing to judge the actions of others without the facts. He'd been tried and hanged more times than he could count in the past few months and he still wondered if he'd done the right thing.

"Dylan showed up as the camp ended and it seemed like he was in great shape. He asked me to join him on this camping trip in the Cascades. We spent a week up there just hanging out, watching the snow melt. It was a good time. When the season started we had to go through the usual evaluation junk, medical checks, you know the drill."

Josie nodded watching him closely.

"Everything seemed fine with him," Trevor paused. "I grabbed his gear bag one day looking for my knife. We were always mixing up our stuff. I found one of those little can things of mints and I popped one in my mouth. They weren't mints. Dylan came in the tent and saw the can on top of his bag. He tried to be casual about it but we had a big fight and I made him tell me the truth."

Josie looked confused.

"How did he hide it from the drug screening?" she asked.

Trevor sighed.

"On our camping trip, we were snowed in a couple of times. We were using water bottles to, uh, you know..."

Josie nodded.

"He kept one of the bottles I'd used and found a way to slip it in."

"So you turned him in," Josie surmised the rest. "I see what my Dad meant when he said you'd scared them by doing the right thing."

"Mitch said that?" Trevor asked with a surprised look on his face. "I had no idea how much Joe told him. I didn't tell anyone. Dylan said I'd ruined his life over nothing. He couldn't seem to understand how he was putting everyone else at risk. I don't even know where he went after that."

The two of them fell silent as they were both lost in their own thoughts about the risks they took to do a job that demanded everything of them. The quiet in the cabin was matched by the silence outside as the storm moved on, leaving them cleansed of the past.

Chapter Five

Back at base camp, Mitch paced back and forth as he waited for the teams to report back in with their findings. The storm forced the crew to spend the night pinned down at the safe zone. They watched the fire lose momentum and eventually begin to fall back. The torrential rain saturated the black, turning it into a mushy bog of ash and mud. It was nearly morning before he was able to send out a search party to look for Josie and Trevor.

Jake and Brian were the first to head out along the river to look for any signs of them. They quickly returned with the melted radio and charred gear they'd found on the bank of the river.

"We know they made it to the river," Jake said to his father. "It's possible they found a way across and they're on the other side. I suggest we call in an air search along the river as soon as they're able to get up."

Stepping in close to his father so only he could hear, Jake added, "Josie's fine. I know it. We'll find her. There's nothing to worry about."

Mitch studied his son's face carefully, wanting to believe in that strange twin connection that existed between them. His heart agreed because any other outcome was unthinkable. Josie was as capable as any other man on his crew. She would have found a way to escape the fire. He also believed in Trevor, as the young man had proven his own resourcefulness many times over the last few weeks. More so than that, he'd proven he cared for Josie and this counted for a lot with Mitch.

As the other teams brought back their reports on the status of the fire, he turned his attention back to the job at hand. The heavy rain had accomplished far more in one day then they'd been able to do in a month. Once Josie and Trevor were found, they just might be looking at the end of this one. There was a cautious sense of optimism in the air as the crew made its way back to their main camp. The rest of the search would be handled from the air.

***

Josie realized the storm had long since passed and her stomach was growling loudly. She jumped up and checked her now dry jump suit before getting dressed. Trevor was quick to follow her lead and they hurried outside to check out their surroundings. The path they'd followed in the storm appeared to be the only access to the cabin. The rough trail didn't appear on Josie's map.

"We might as well head back up the trail until we can get a sighting on something or find a cross trail," Josie suggested. "I'm not too keen on another rafting trip today."

The two of them started walking back in the direction they'd come the day before. They hadn't gone very far when Josie darted off the trail and fell to her knees.

At first Trevor thought she was sick or something but then he realized she was cramming something into her mouth.

"What are you eating," he demanded, followed by, "and were you going to share with me?"

Josie turned to look at him with a big blue grin on her face. She held out a handful of blueberries toward him. He hurried to join her as they scrambled and ate their way through a decent breakfast of fresh berries. Sated, they both sat back on their haunches and looked around for any more of the fruit.

Trevor saw some heavily laden branches of red berries and pointed them out to her. She shook her head no and made a face.

"Not even the birds touch those around here," she said, "and it's too early for most of the other kinds that are good to eat. The blueberries always come first up here."

"Any chance of finding a granola bar bush?" he grinned at her.

She threw a stick at him and jumped up.

"Not on your life," she shouted over her shoulder as she took off down the trail.

Once again Trevor found himself trying to keep

up with her. They hadn't run very far when Josie stopped in a small clearing and took a look around. Pulling out her map, she knelt down and ran her finger over the line of peaks comparing it to the view she now had of the mountains.

"I'm pretty sure we're in this area," she said thoughtfully, "and there's a fire road that runs across this trail leading down to the river. We can follow the road to get to the top of the tree line and set up a marker for the search planes."

"Or, we can go back down to the river," Trevor said, "build another raft and float down to this village here."

"Won't work," Josie countered. "No rope. No tools."

"What are the chances the search planes will be looking for us above the tree line," Trevor asked in self-defense. "And how are we going to build a marker without any tools?"

"You've got a knife. I just don't see you cutting down any trees with it big enough to float us down the river, but we can build a marker with branches."

Taken aback by her logic, Trevor was forced to agree hers was a better plan and they set off down the trail at a more measured pace, given the distance they now knew they needed to cover that day. Both of them hoped to be back at camp by supper time. Josie knew Mitch would have search planes in the air as soon as they were cleared to fly.

Unfortunately, she miscalculated where the search would begin based on their last known location. Neither of them took that into consideration as they walked on down the trail, keeping an eye out for large moose. Nobody was thinking of bears.

They hadn't traveled for very long when they reached the point where the fire road crossed the trail. Both of them stopped and took a hard look in every direction. There was nothing to distinguish one direction from any other that they could see.

"I still think the river is a better option," Trevor said firmly. "We can find a way downriver to that village. I'm sure of it."

"Well, I'm in charge," Josie argued, "and we're not going that way."

Trevor almost laughed as it looked as if she was about to stamp her foot and pout...almost, wisely, he decided to be quiet and follow her lead. As she said, she was the one in charge. He fell in behind her as she started up the fire road. They'd walked for nearly an hour when Josie stopped suddenly causing Trevor to bump into her. He reached out to steady her as she began walking backwards forcing him to step back.

"What is it?" he whispered.

She leaned to the side and cleared his line of sight. The mama bear and her cub were enjoying their own breakfast a stone's throw ahead of them. Fortunately, they were downwind of her and she hadn't spotted them yet. Josie motioned for him to back up slowly while holding her finger to her lips for silence. Trevor was happy to follow her lead. Bear encounters out in the wild didn't always go well for the humans involved. He was sure he'd used up all of his luck on the last one.

They managed to slip back down the road and out of sight around a corner before either of them took a real breath. Trevor could feel the sweat trickling down the middle of his back. Josie sat down on a fallen tree and took another look at her map. The river was suddenly looking like a better option but she hated to admit it to Trevor. She also wasn't that inclined to getting back into the water. However, facing a mama bear was even less attractive. Trevor watched her carefully as she made her decision.

"Looks like the river might be a better option," she said carefully avoiding his gaze. "Let's hope there's nothing between us and the water."

Trevor didn't answer as they headed back the way they'd just come. He wasn't one to rub salt into wounded feelings. Scanning the edges of the road as they walked, he noted a lot of saplings he might be able to bind together with strips of bark. He was confident there was a way to build another raft even without his ax. He began to whistle as they went along. Soon Josie joined in and they made a game of guessing each other's tunes. The distraction helped the time to fly and soon the sound of the river began to drown out their music.

Trevor set right to work gathering saplings into a pile. Josie scanned the area and checked the bank for any kind of path they could use. The brush came right down to the edge of the river for as far as she could see in either direction. She groaned as she realized Trevor's plan was their best option. There was no way she was going to admit her fear of being out on the river. She gritted her teeth and turned back to help him.

At that moment, the sound of a plane's engine caught their attention and they both looked up hoping to catch sight of it. The pilot was flying as low over the river as the trees would allow with the spotter hanging out the door scanning the bank on his side. The problem was they were on the opposite bank. Both of them ripped off their jackets and began waving them wildly and shouting.

The pilot caught sight of them and waved back. He made a circle around the area and motioned for them to wait there. The plane turned and headed back up river with a waggle of the wings and a wave from the spotter. Tears came to Josie's eyes as she knew her father was being notified of her location. She felt terrible about the worry he'd endured because of her. She also was relieved to not have to get back into the river. They were both going to get their wish to be back at camp for supper. The two of them sat down to wait.

***

Jake took the call on the radio that Josie and Trevor were spotted. He hurried to let his father know the good news. His relief was evident on his face and Mitch knew they were found the moment he saw his son.

"Are they okay?" Mitch asked.

"Apparently. They were jumping up and down and waving their jackets in the air. The plane spotted them about eighteen miles downriver and the chopper is on its way to pick them up. They should be here within the hour."

Mitch took a deep breath and let it out slowly. He generally avoided conflicts between his children as they always managed to find a way to work things out themselves. This problem, however, he knew was related to him. He decided to step in.

"You want to tell me what's going on between you and your sister?" Mitch asked quietly.

Jake looked pained as he carefully avoided his father's searching gaze. His guilt had grown nearly unbearable with Josie lost in the wilderness. He suspected their disagreement had a lot to do with her disappearance. She wasn't always careful when she was mad.

"She thinks I tricked her," Jake admitted. "I told

SLOW BURN IN THE WILDERNESS

her I was worried about you not being able to continue much longer. I also reminded her of the pact we made to come out together."

"You know I wouldn't hold either of you to that, don't you?" Mitch asked quietly.

"I know," Jake said sadly, "but I also know Josie's the real reason you've stayed in this long. You feel like you have to watch over her."

Mitch's eyes stung as he heard Jake's words. He'd never considered himself as playing favorites with his children but there was an element of truth in his son's thinking. He never worried about Jake in the way he worried about Josie.

"It's not that I don't love you, son," Mitch replied.

"I know. I get it. I worry about her too. That's why I'd like her to get out and do something else while she still can. Being a fire fighter is all I know and like you, it's what I want, but she only ever wanted to do whatever we're doing."

"We have to let her make her own decision Jake."

"I know. Let's just hope she makes a good one."

***

When the chopper landed at the air strip, the entire crew was on hand to celebrate the return of their missing teammates. Trevor was embarrassed at all the hoopla and tried to escape to his tent but the men would have none of it. Josie was quick to lead them all back to the mess tent where she proceeded to eat a half dozen granola bars. Brian was cooking up a batch of chili and everyone gathered around to hear the story of their little adventure.

Mitch put on his crew boss face and looked at her sternly as she relayed how the fire had cut them off. Trevor's raft building skills earned him a few cheers and everyone pitched in to talk about the fierce storm. Their night in the ramshackle trapper's cabin was carefully glossed over and the story of their encounter with the mama bear took center stage. Soon they were all laughing and talking over bowls of chili. No one noticed when Trevor slipped away. He knew things between him and Josie couldn't go back to business as usual. His feelings for her were dominating his thoughts. He just didn't know what to do about it.

On his way back from the latrine, he found Jake blocking his way. Trevor hesitated as he tried to figure out the larger man's thoughts. He was surprised when Jake stuck out his hand. He almost flinched thinking Jake was about to hit him, but Jake took his hand and gave him a firm shake.

"Thanks for watching out for my sister," Jake said kindly. "I know she can be a bit of a handful."

Trevor nodded at a loss for words and waited.

"She likes you," Jake added. "You know that, don't you?"

Trevor stared at Jake in surprise. He wanted more than anything to believe that.

"And how do you feel about that?" Trevor asked slowly.

"I think it's great," Jake replied, swatting him on the shoulder.

"As do I," came a voice from behind them.

They both turned to find Mitch standing there watching them.

Trevor flushed at the idea they were both watching him and gauging his intentions towards Josie. He wondered how she would feel if she knew about this little discussion in the woods. It was a pretty good bet she'd be mad.

"So what are you going to do about it?" Jake asked with a grin.

Trevor shrugged.

"This is a whole new area for me," he confessed. "I'm still trying to figure it out."

"Well, don't take too long," Mitch replied. "She's not the kind of woman to wait around for anyone."

"Boy, do I know that," Trevor laughed. "I spent most of my time out there trying to keep up."

The three men laughed in agreement as they all knew the truth of those words.

SLOW BURN IN THE WILDERNESS

Chapter Six

The rain continued off and on for the next couple of weeks and the fire reached the stage of being declared contained. The crew spent their time checking for hotspots and cleaning up the camp in preparation for moving on. They knew it would be time to go when the fire was put into monitor status and everyone started to make plans for a brief respite before their next deployment. There was always another fire in the future for them.

One evening, Josie was fresh from the slough and rubbing a towel over her head. She'd found a new sense of excitement in her budding relationship with Trevor. The two of them sat together at meals and worked side by side during the day. He hadn't tried to kiss her yet, but there were moments when she was sure he was about to just before he turned away. The rest of the crew were watching them and waiting in anticipation much to their chagrin.

She started to get dressed for supper when the blouse her father had given her caught her eye. She picked it up and held it to her cheek trying to imagine Trevor's face when he saw her wearing it. Her breath caught in her throat. She'd never worn anything like this in the camp before and the men were all sure to notice. Suddenly, she didn't care and throwing caution to the wind, she put it on.

As the soft folds of silky cloth enveloped her curves, a flush came to her face. She brushed out her hair and left it to lay on her shoulders. There weren't any mirrors here to show her the picture she presented, but in her mind's eye, she knew. Her feet slipped quietly over the trail as she felt herself almost floating on air, giddy with anticipation.

When she stepped into the main tent, it appeared as if the whole crew was already gathered for supper. It took a few moments for everyone to notice her, but as each man caught sight of her, they fell silent in appreciation. Josie's eyes scanned the group eagerly looking for the one person that truly mattered. She realized two things in the same moment. Every eye in the room was fixated on her and Trevor wasn't there.

One of the men couldn't contain his appreciation and he let out a low whistle of admiration. Tossing an angry look in his direction, Josie turned to flee back to her tent in embarrassment and frustration. She felt horrified that she'd given into her feelings and exposed herself before the crew. There was no way she was going to let them see her do something like that ever again. In her haste to get away, she ran blindly down the path to her tent. Tears tickled at the corners of her eyes.

The sudden impact of two bodies in motion caused both of them to grunt in surprise. Trevor reached out to grab for Josie as she bounced off his chest. Stunned, she grabbed onto his arms, pulling him close as she struggled to stay upright.

"Where's the fire?" Trevor asked in amusement, as he leaned back to look at her.

Josie turned her face away to hide her embarrassment. He reached out and cupped her chin in his hand, forcing her to look at him. He couldn't help but notice the soft fabric of her pink blouse and the lack of the usual ponytail.

Suddenly, he realized this foray into the unexpected was on his behalf and his amusement deepened into appreciation of the beautiful woman standing before him. He leaned towards her still holding her chin in his hand and gently touched his lips to hers. As he felt her respond to his touch, he gathered her close and kissed her again. His heart soared as he felt her kiss him back.

The sound of a stick breaking behind them startled them both and they jumped apart. Turning around, they found themselves alone. They looked back at each other and began to smile deeply.

"I was just heading over for supper," Trevor said with a grin. "Would you care to join me? I hear there's plenty of tuna left to eat."

Josie made a face before taking the arm he was holding out to her. She knew in that moment, she would follow this man anywhere. The two of them walked back to the main tent.

When they appeared, the rest of the crew tried to

act nonchalant as if nothing unusual was taking place. The man who'd embarrassed himself by whistling was covered with red welts and it was clear he'd taken a bit of a pummeling on her behalf. They helped themselves to food and made their way over to sit next to her father and brother. No one missed the flush on both of their faces and money began to change hands around the tables.

"What's going on?" Josie asked innocently as she became aware of the exchanges.

"Oh. Some of the crew started a pool taking bets on how long it was going to take the two of you to kiss each other," Jake said with a grin. "Winning required a witness and apparently, there was a sighting."

Josie cast a look of disdain over the crew as they carefully avoided her eye. Her father and brother caught her attention as Jake slid a five dollar bill across the table to his father. Mitch was quick to shove it into his pocket.

"You too?" Josie exclaimed in mock horror.

She shook her head and buried her face in her hands. Trevor laughed as he realized they'd been watched carefully for the last few days. He was relieved that their feelings for each other were out in the open. He dug into his supper with a new appetite. *My life has just taken a major change for the better,* he thought, with a deep sense of contentment.

***

The next morning, Trevor was up early as he woke up with an overwhelming sense of excitement to see what the new day would bring. He hurried to dress and headed over to the main tent for breakfast. Brian was in his usual perch with a rifle across his back and a bowl of beans in front of him. When he saw Trevor, he gave him a sour look and leaned over his bowl.

"Good morning, Brian," Trevor said brightly. "Seen any bears around here today?"

Brian made a growling sound as he shoved a large spoonful of beans into his mouth as an answer. Trevor figured that was the best he was going to get and began to gather his usual morning foodstuffs. He was too happy to get offended over the big guy's reticence.

"It isn't fair," Brian mumbled through a mouthful of beans.

Trevor paused and came over to sit down next to him.

"What isn't fair?"

"I've been in love with her for two years," Brian muttered, "and you waltz in here and steal her heart in a little over two months. It's not fair!"

Trevor froze as he considered what Brian was saying. He had no idea the big guy was soft on Josie and he was willing to bet she didn't know either. He struggled to think of something helpful to say in response to a clearly broken heart. Brian continued to eat beans refusing to look at Trevor.

"Brian," Trevor said, "you really like beans, don't you?"

Brian nodded sadly.

"Have you ever seen Josie eating beans?"

Brian paused considering the matter before shaking his head no.

"You see. She's not into beans. I would think that means she's just not the right woman for you. What do you think?"

Brian was silent as he sat there chewing a mouthful of beans. Trevor left him to his thoughts as he finished throwing together his own breakfast. The two of them ate in silence as the rest of the crew began to show up. Trevor couldn't gauge what effect his words had on Brian, but the matter never came up between them again.

***

"When we get to Fairbanks," Trevor asked hesitantly, "will you go on a real date with me?"

"Just one," Josie teased.

"I thought we'd start with dinner and work our way around through all the other things a normal couple does when they're starting a relationship."

"Starting?" Josie questioned. "I'd say we're already in a relationship and forget normal. I like things the way they already are between us."

"What do you mean?" Trevor asked.

"I'm the boss," Josie began, "and you have to do what I say..."

She broke off laughing as he grabbed her and began to tickle her mercilessly.

"Okay! Okay! I take it back," she exclaimed, pulling away from him.

"How many dates do I have to take you on before you'll say yes?" Trevor asked with a glint in his eye.

"Yes to what?" Josie asked looking confused.

"You know. Yes to the question," Trevor probed, reaching out to pull her into his arms.

Josie's eyes grew wide with surprise. She stared at him trying to see if he was still playing with her or if he was serious. The intense look in his eyes was all the answer she needed.

"I think we're already past that point," she said slyly looking up at him.

He responded with a gentle kiss that took her breath away. Neither of them noticed Mitch watching them from the other side of the airstrip. The smile on his face said it all.

SLOW BURN IN THE WILDERNESS

Epilogue

Josie adjusted her veil for the tenth time as she turned around in front of the mirror again. Her brother stood at the window watching the crowd gathered below on the terrace. He knew it was past time to go down but he wasn't ready to give up this time of having her all to himself. Once she was married, he would slip aside as a brother must while her husband took center stage. A knock came at the door and he stepped over to open it a crack.

"Is there a problem?" Mitch asked from the other side of the door. "Everyone's waiting downstairs."

"No. No problem, Dad," Josie called. "I'm trying to get used to seeing myself in a dress."

"Well, don't take all day about it," he called back. "It's not like you have to wear it forever. You can put your jeans back on after the wedding if you want."

Josie smoothed her hands down the front of her mother's wedding dress. She'd never imagined herself wearing the frilly frock at her own wedding. The sight of herself as a bride was overwhelming but not for any specific reason. Her relationship with Trevor had given her new insights into the joy and beauty of being a woman. She felt herself blossoming as he poured out his love upon her.

"You look incredible," Jake said as he closed the

door. "I'm sure Trevor will think so too."

Josie sighed as her thoughts turned to Trevor waiting below and then she laughed.

"Trevor would think I looked incredible if I showed up in yellow Kevlar and a fire hat," Josie said with a big grin. "In fact, I wouldn't be surprised if that was what half the crowd down there is wearing today."

"You'd lose that bet. I'm looking at a lot of black suits and nothing in Kevlar or yellow for that matter. Now are you ready to go down or should I let them know you're not coming?"

Turning to her brother, Josie smiled at him and nodded her head.

"I'm ready for the rest of my life to begin," she said walking to the door where her father waited to walk her downstairs. "Let's get this show on the road!"

THE END

About The Author

Renee Hart is the author of the Alaska Adventure Romance series. She writes clean Alaskan adventure romance and romantic comedy. Renee lives in the Alaskan Bush with her husband and their dog and cat. When she's not writing or getting firewood ready for the winter, you can find her quilting, baking bread or sipping hot cocoa by the wood stove with a good book.

Check out her Facebook page at

https://www.facebook.com/ReneeHartAuthor/

SLOW BURN IN THE WILDERNESS

Books by Renee Hart

A Single Year In The Bush (Book 1)

A Summer Nanny In Fairbanks (Book 2)

A River Home (Book 2.1)

Homer: End Of The Road (Book 3)

Together In The Wild (Book 4)

Something Wild In Anchorage (Book 5)

Touched By The Northern Lights (Book 5.5)

Yesterday Island (Book 6)

Slow Burn In The Wilderness (Book 7)

available on Amazon.com

I hope you enjoyed this story.
If you would leave a review on Amazon
it would be greatly appreciated!

Sincerely,
Renee Hart